D0573622

PURCHASED FROM
MULTNOMAH COUNTY LIBRARY
TITLE WAVE BOOKSTORE

SOMEWHERE IN AFRICA

by Ingrid Mennen and Niki Daly
illustrated by Nicolaas Maritz

DUTTON CHILDREN'S BOOKS
NEW YORK

Ashraf lives in Africa...

not Africa where lions
laze in golden grass,

not Africa where crocodiles glide through
muddy rivers, silent and hungry,

not Africa where zebras
gallop over great plains.

Ashraf lives in a city,
a city at the very tip of
the great African continent.

Ashraf *has* seen Africa
wild and untamed,
captured in a book
borrowed from the
city library.

In summer, the city lies soaked in African sun,
dry under endless blue sky.

Ashraf loves his city. Deep black shadows
cut across pavements and streets.

Traffic lights blink as noisy cars and
city people come and go.

Ashraf knows his city.
He zigzags
down its alleys

and jumps over its cracks.

He stops at The Lizard to see the truck
made from old Coca-Cola cans.

Next door is the strange shop that sells ancient tusks
and tortoises and a stool with elephant toes.

Ashraf knows the crazy songs
of the fruit seller:
 "Onions make you cry,
  Bananas make you sigh,
  Mangoes where woman goes
  And so do I,"
he sings, as Ashraf goes by.

Flower sellers sit smiling between the
agapanthus and the everlastings.

Next to the supermarket is the place where
drummers drum almost forgotten stories

and dancers dance to the music
that explodes from marimba and horn.
That is the music of Africa.

Ashraf watches his shadow shrink as the sun moves right above him. It is midday, time for him to take his favorite book back to the big city library.

The library is quiet and cool, with a jungle of books to choose from. Slowly, Ashraf stalks the shelves for something special. Something wild and untamed.

Mrs. Mackenzie, the librarian, smiles. She knows what's going to happen next.

"The same one, please," asks Ashraf as he hands over his old book, his favorite book, to be renewed.

Outside, the sun
is getting hotter,
so Ashraf walks
on the shady side
of the street
all the way home.

Somewhere in Africa,
Ashraf knows,
lions are lazing
in tall golden grass
and overhead
this same hot sun
is shining down on them.

For the children of the Bo-Kaap, Cape Town
–I.M., –N.D., –N.M.

Text copyright © 1990 by Ingrid Mennen and Niki Daly
Illustrations copyright © 1990 by Nicolaas Maritz

All rights reserved.

CIP Data is available.

First published in the United States 1992 by
Dutton Children's Books,
a division of Penguin Books USA Inc.

Originally published in South Africa by
Songololo Books, a division of David Philip Publishers (Pty) Ltd.
208 Werdmuller Centre, Claremont, 7700 South Africa

First American Edition   Printed in Hong Kong

10 9 8 7 6 5 4

ISBN 0-525-44848-9